POWER PACK

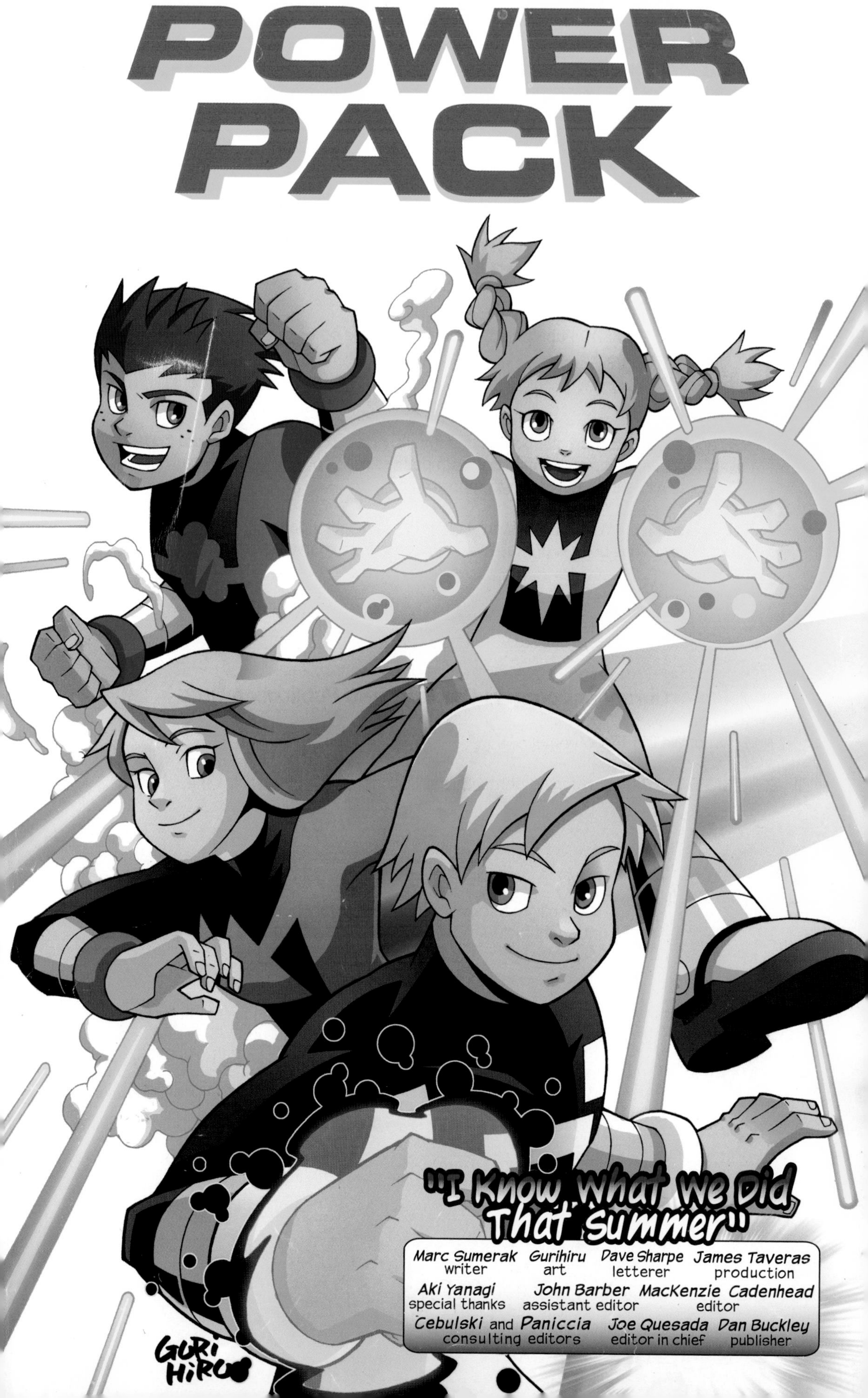
"I Know What We Did That Summer"
Marc Sumerak writer
Gurihiru art
Dave Sharpe letterer
James Taveras production
Aki Yanagi special thanks
John Barber assistant editor
MacKenzie Cadenhead editor
Cebulski and Paniccia consulting editors
Joe Quesada editor in chief
Dan Buckley publisher
GURI HIRU

VISIT US AT
www.abdopub.com

Spotlight, a division of ABDO Publishing Company Inc., is the school and library distributor of the Marvel Entertainment books.

Library bound edition © 2006

Library of Congress Cataloging-in-Publication Data

I Know What We Did That Summer

ISBN 1-59961-033-7   (Reinforced Library Bound Edition)

All Spotlight books are reinforced library binding and manufactured in the United States of America

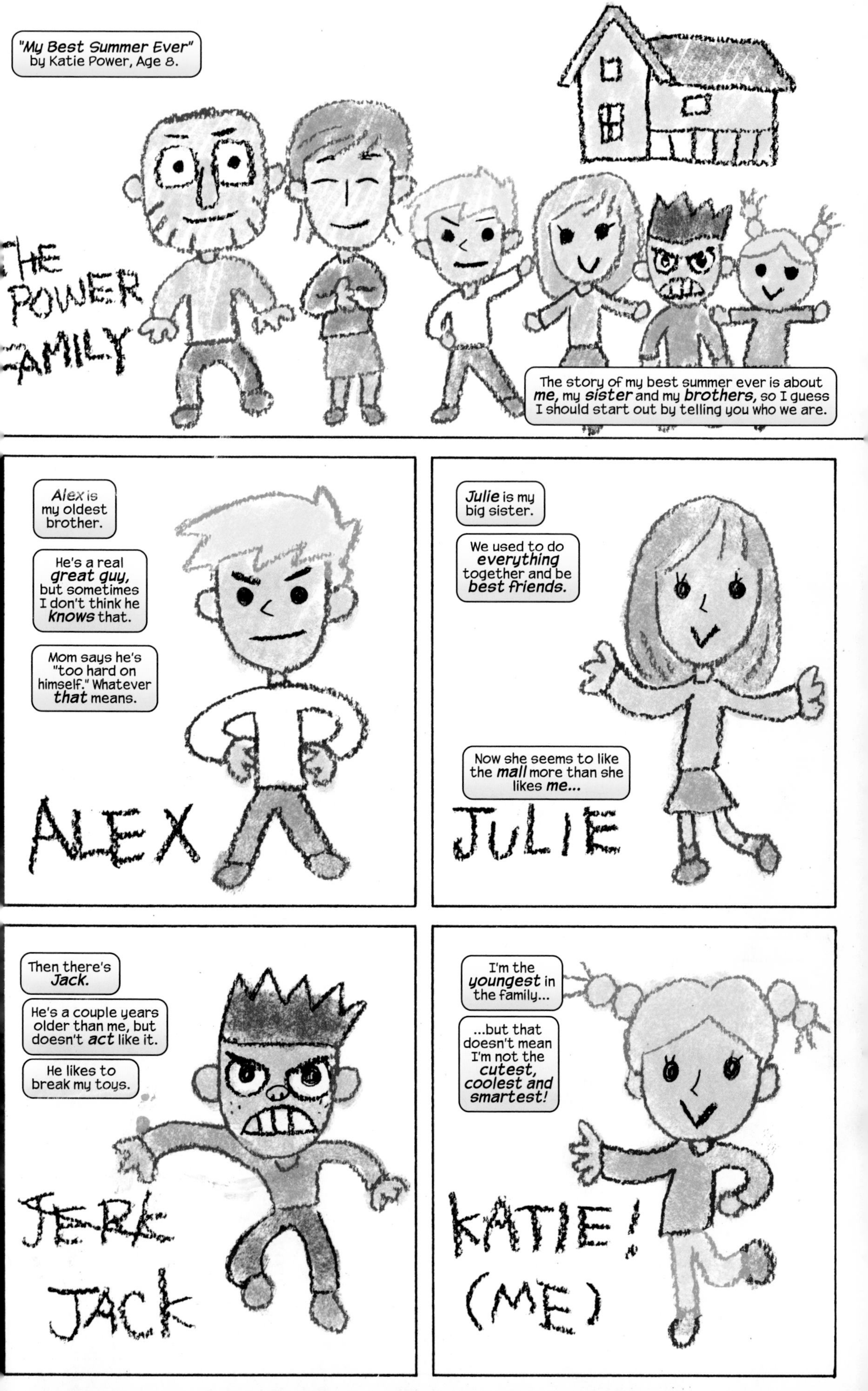
"My Best Summer Ever" by Katie Power, Age 8.
THE POWER FAMILY
The story of my best summer ever is about me, my sister and my brothers, so I guess I should start out by telling you who we are.
Alex is my oldest brother.
He's a real great guy, but sometimes I don't think he knows that.
Mom says he's "too hard on himself." Whatever that means.
ALEX
Julie is my big sister.
We used to do everything together and be best friends.
Now she seems to like the mall more than she likes me...
JULIE
Then there's Jack.
He's a couple years older than me, but doesn't act like it.
He likes to break my toys.
~~JERK~~
JACK
I'm the youngest in the family...
...but that doesn't mean I'm not the cutest, coolest and smartest!
KATIE!
(ME)

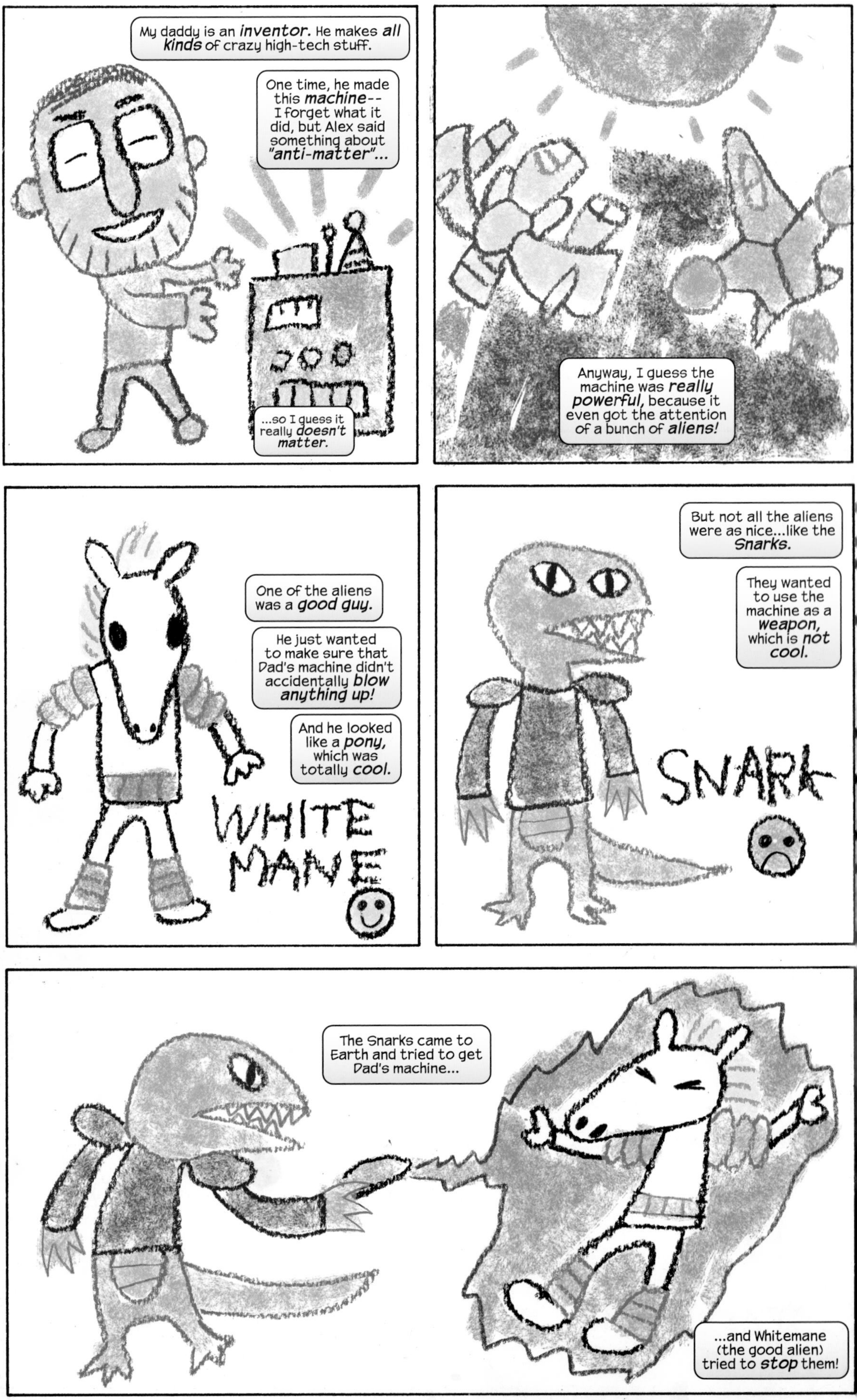
My daddy is an inventor. He makes all kinds of crazy high-tech stuff.
One time, he made this machine-- I forget what it did, but Alex said something about "anti-matter"...
...so I guess it really doesn't matter.
Anyway, I guess the machine was really powerful, because it even got the attention of a bunch of aliens!
One of the aliens was a good guy.
He just wanted to make sure that Dad's machine didn't accidentally blow anything up!
And he looked like a pony, which was totally cool.
WHITE MANE
But not all the aliens were as nice...like the Snarks.
They wanted to use the machine as a weapon, which is not cool.
SNARK
The Snarks came to Earth and tried to get Dad's machine...
...and Whitemane (the good alien) tried to stop them!

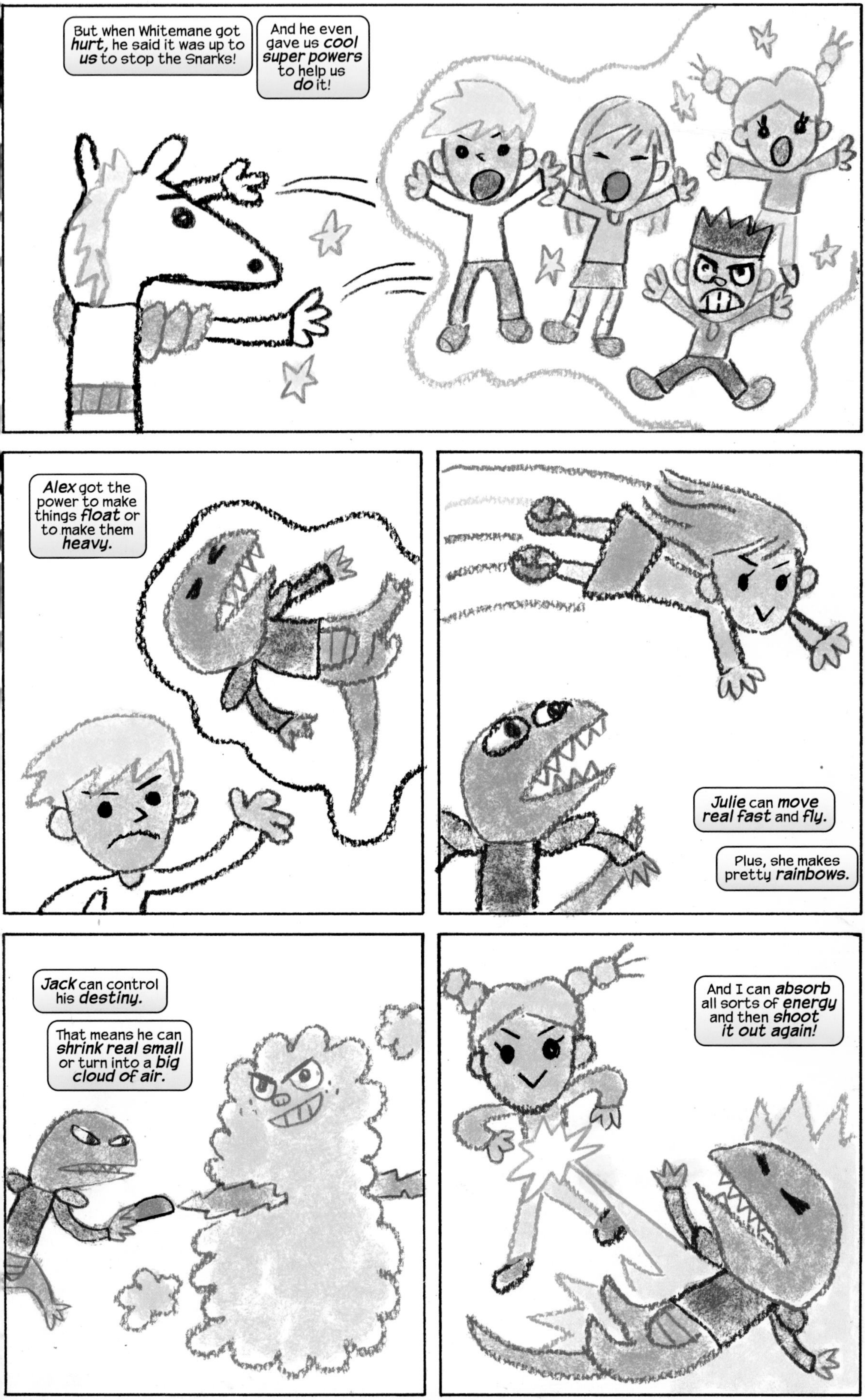
But when Whitemane got *hurt*, he said it was up to *us* to stop the Snarks!
And he even gave us *cool super powers* to help us *do* it!
Alex got the power to make things *float* or to make them *heavy.*
Julie can *move real fast* and *fly.*
Plus, she makes pretty *rainbows.*
Jack can control his *destiny.*
That means he can *shrink real small* or turn into a *big cloud of air.*
And I can *absorb* all sorts of *energy* and then *shoot it out again!*

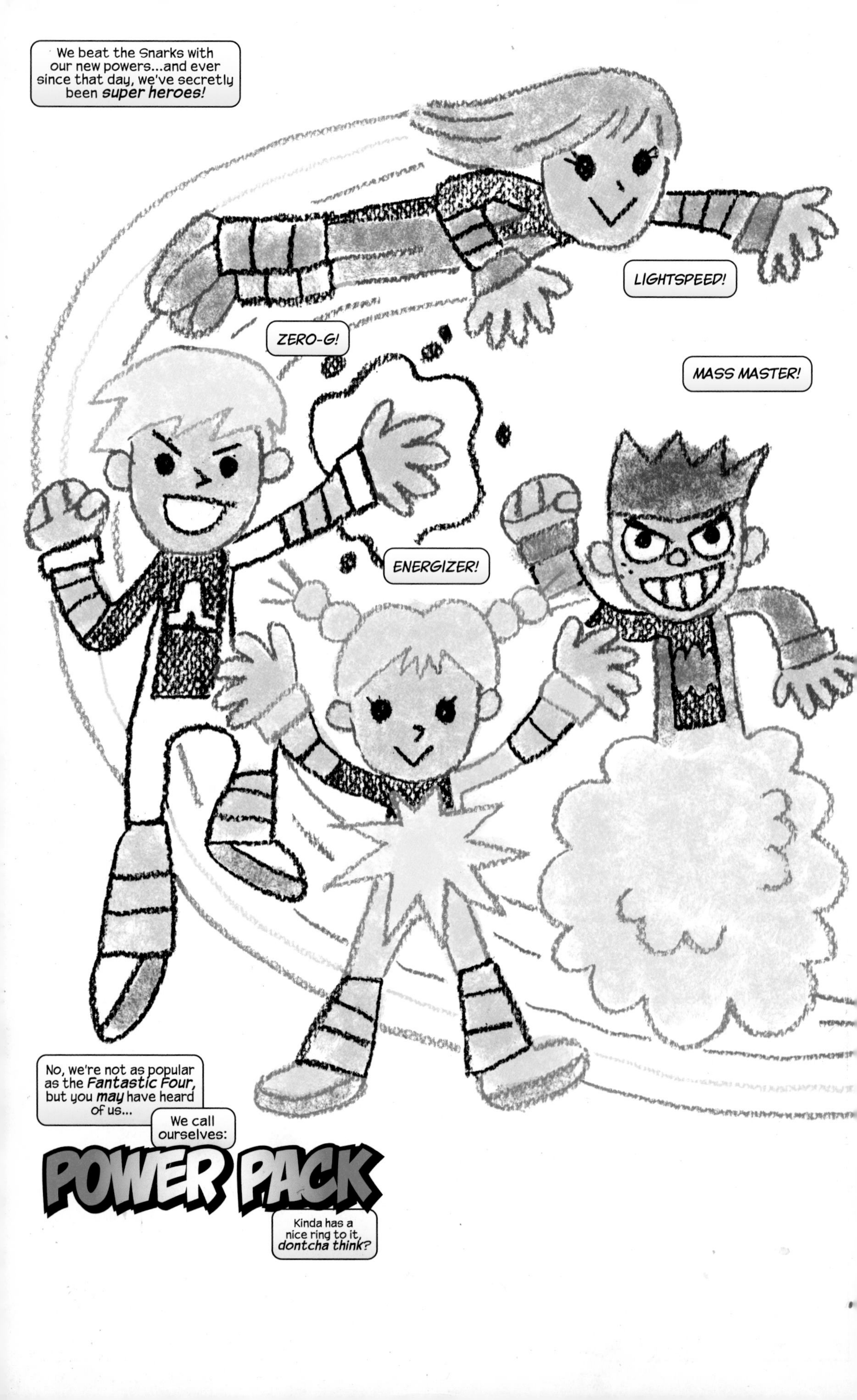

We beat the Snarks with our new powers...and ever since that day, we've secretly been *super heroes!*
LIGHTSPEED!
ZERO-G!
MASS MASTER!
ENERGIZER!
No, we're not as popular as the *Fantastic Four,* but you *may* have heard of us...
We call ourselves:
POWER PACK
Kinda has a nice ring to it, *dontcha think?*

So...what do you guys *think*?

Yeah. I thought it was pretty good *too.*

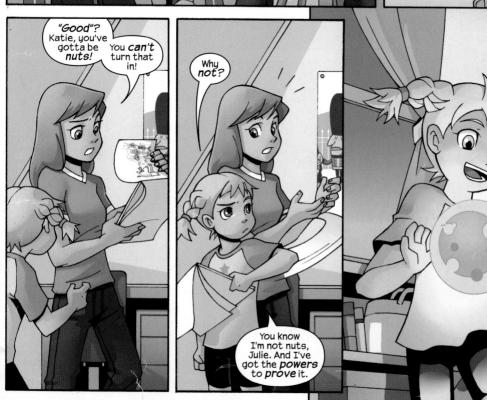

"*Good*"? Katie, you've gotta be *nuts!* You *can't* turn that in!

Why *not*?

You know I'm not nuts, Julie. And I've got the *powers* to *prove* it.

ZEE?

WHITE MANE

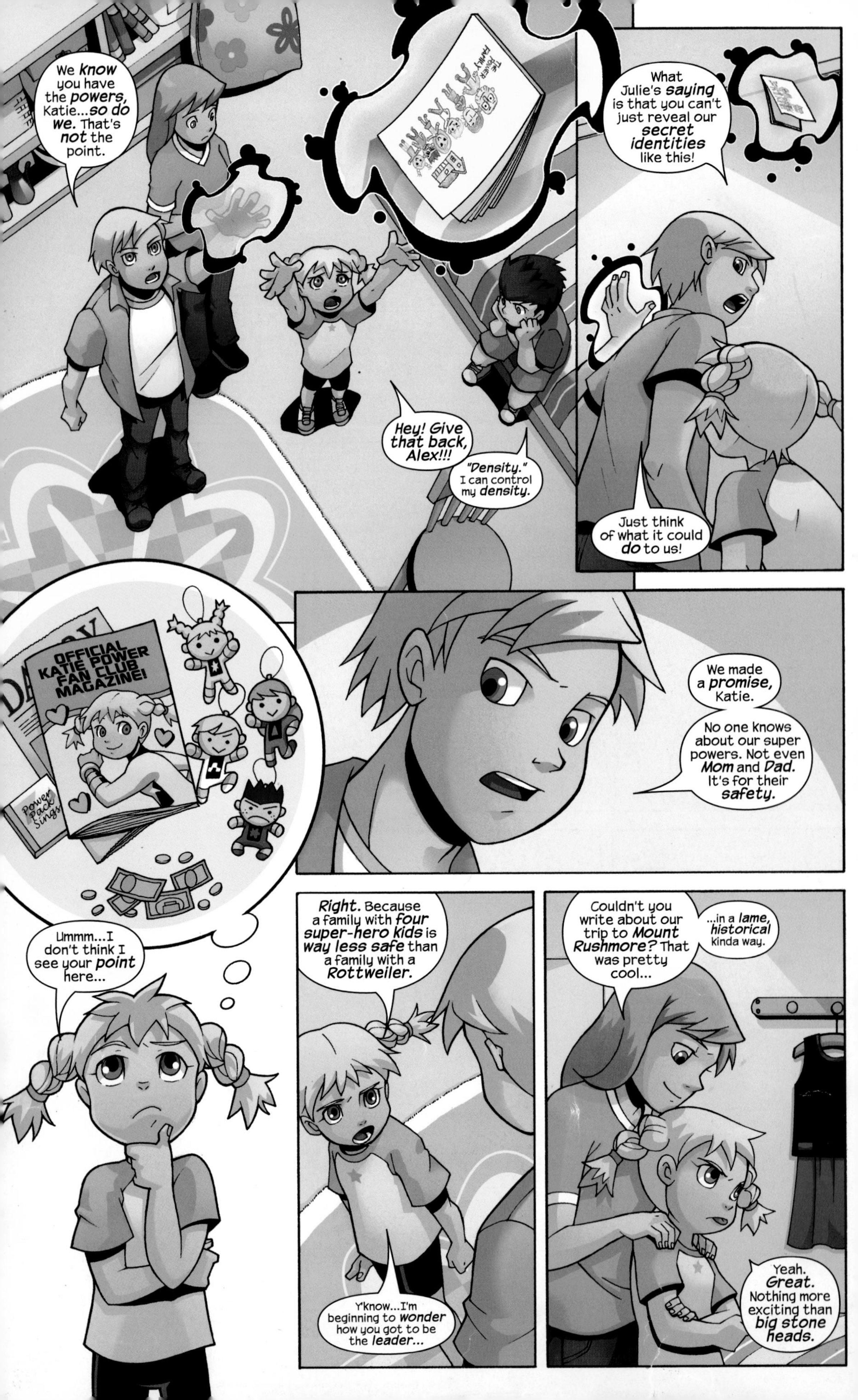
We know you have the powers, Katie...so do we. That's not the point.
THE POWER FAMILY
What Julie's saying is that you can't just reveal our secret identities like this!
Hey! Give that back, Alex!!!
"Density." I can control my density.
Just think of what it could do to us!
OFFICIAL KATIE POWER FAN CLUB MAGAZINE!
Power Pack Sings
We made a promise, Katie.
No one knows about our super powers. Not even Mom and Dad. It's for their safety.
Ummm...I don't think I see your point here...
Right. Because a family with four super-hero kids is way less safe than a family with a Rottweiler.
Y'know...I'm beginning to wonder how you got to be the leader...
Couldn't you write about our trip to Mount Rushmore? That was pretty cool...
...in a lame, historical kinda way.
Yeah. Great. Nothing more exciting than big stone heads.

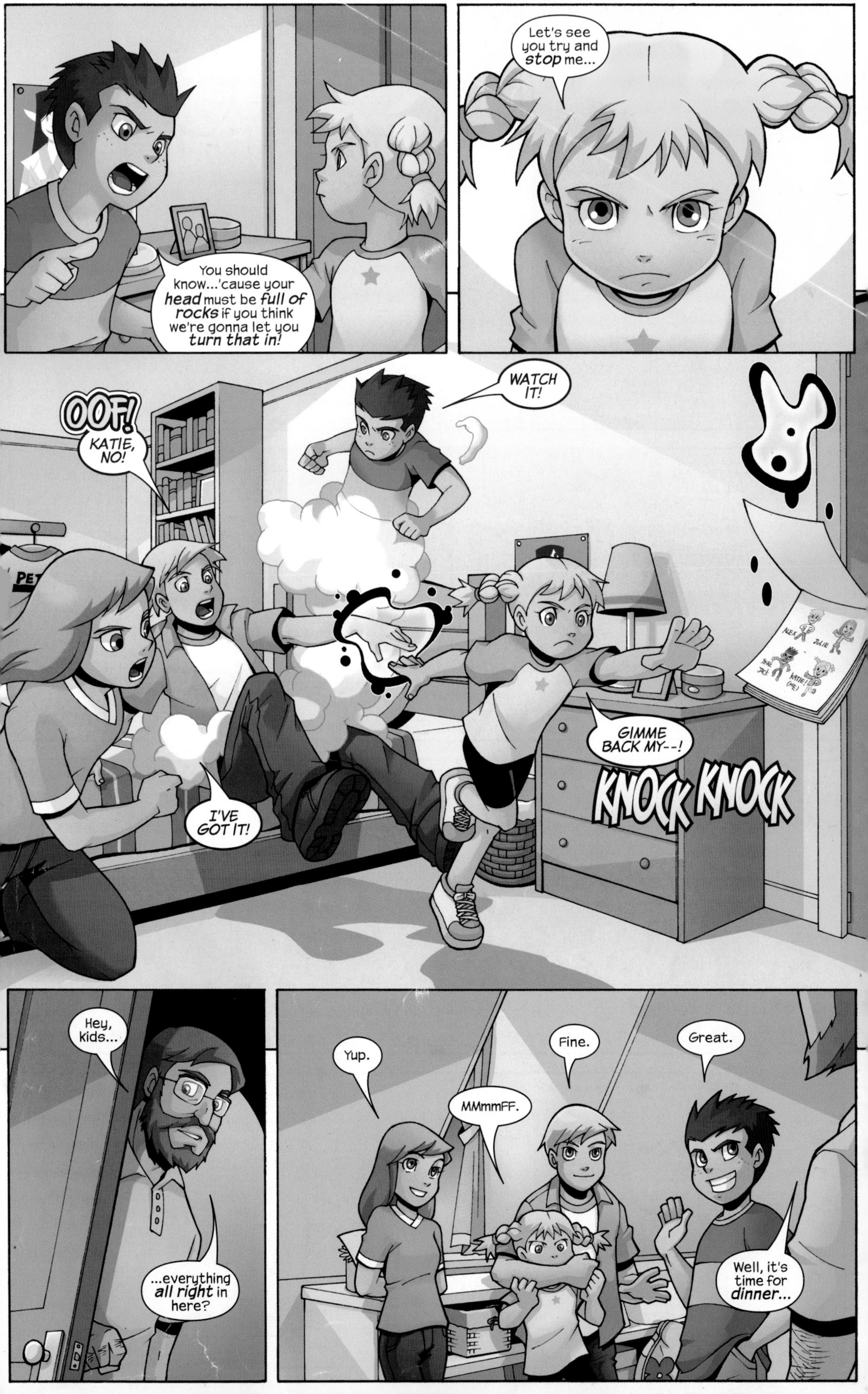
You should know...'cause your head must be full of rocks if you think we're gonna let you turn that in!
Let's see you try and stop me...
OOF!
KATIE, NO!
WATCH IT!
I'VE GOT IT!
GIMME BACK MY--!
KNOCK KNOCK
Hey, kids...
...everything all right in here?
Yup.
MMmmFF.
Fine.
Great.
Well, it's time for dinner...

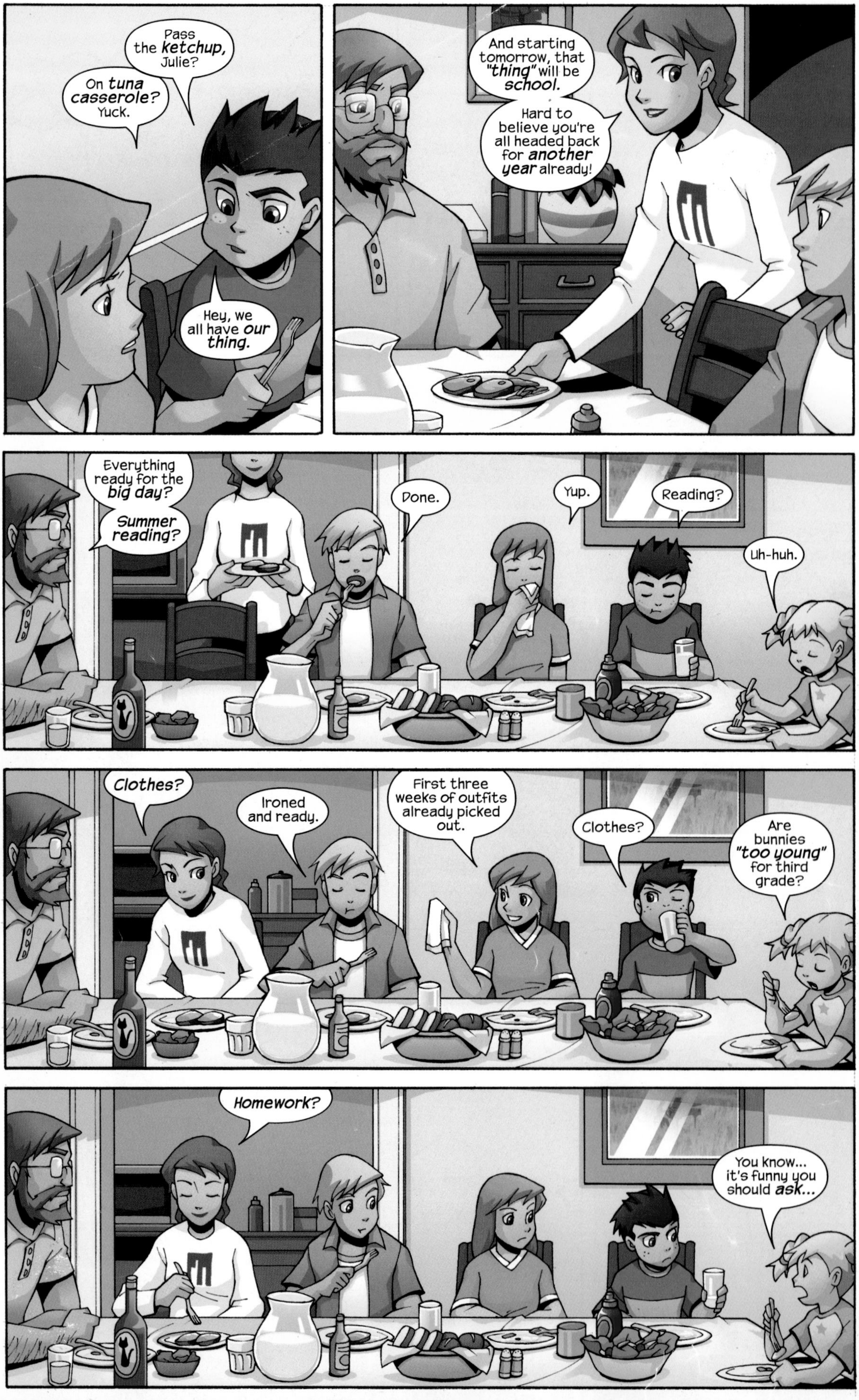
On tuna casserole? Yuck.
Pass the ketchup, Julie?
Hey, we all have our thing.
And starting tomorrow, that "thing" will be school.
Hard to believe you're all headed back for another year already!
Everything ready for the big day?
Summer reading?
Done.
Yup.
Reading?
Uh-huh.
Clothes?
Ironed and ready.
First three weeks of outfits already picked out.
Clothes?
Are bunnies "too young" for third grade?
Homework?
You know... it's funny you should ask...

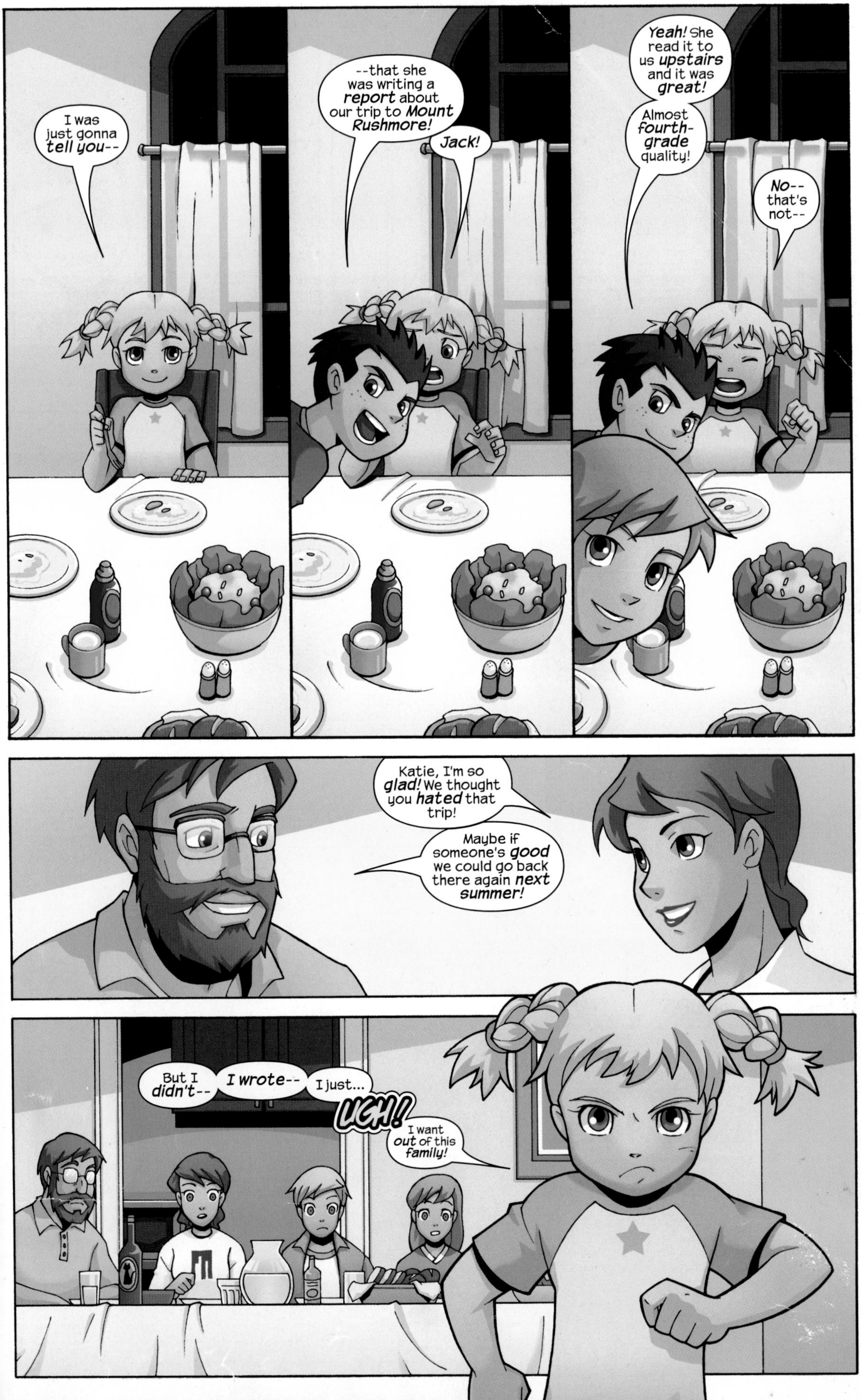
I was just gonna tell you--
--that she was writing a report about our trip to Mount Rushmore!
Jack!
Yeah! She read it to us upstairs and it was great!
Almost fourth-grade quality!
No--that's not--
Katie, I'm so glad! We thought you hated that trip!
Maybe if someone's good we could go back there again next summer!
But I didn't--
I wrote--
I just...
UGH!
I want out of this family!

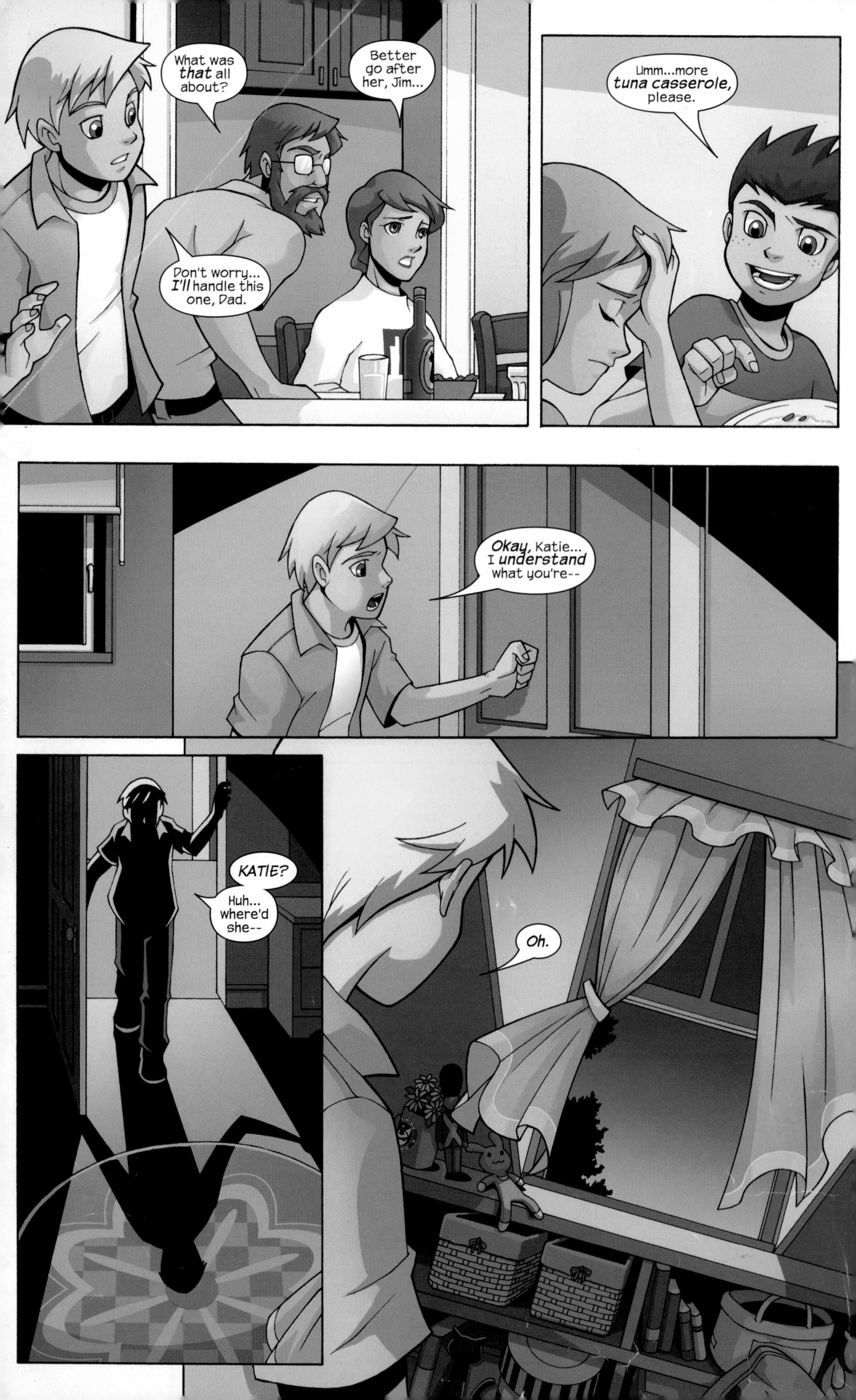
What was that all about?
Better go after her, Jim...
Don't worry... I'll handle this one, Dad.
Umm...more tuna casserole, please.
Okay, Katie... I understand what you're--
KATIE?
Huh... where'd she--
Oh.

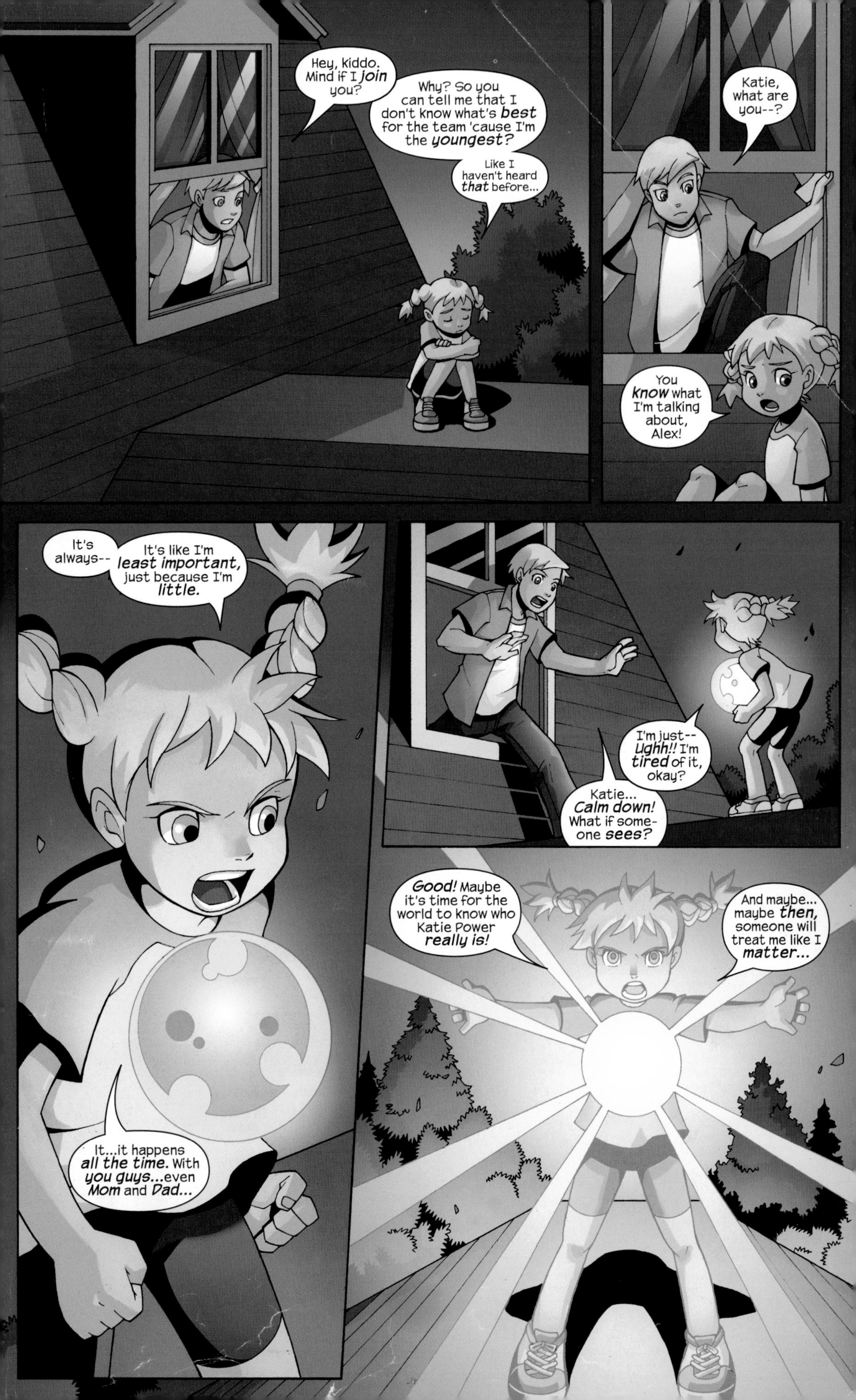
Hey, kiddo. Mind if I join you?
Why? So you can tell me that I don't know what's best for the team 'cause I'm the youngest?
Like I haven't heard that before...
Katie, what are you--?
You know what I'm talking about, Alex!
It's always--
It's like I'm least important, just because I'm little.
It...it happens all the time. With you guys...even Mom and Dad...
I'm just-- Ughh!! I'm tired of it, okay?
Katie... Calm down! What if some-one sees?
Good! Maybe it's time for the world to know who Katie Power really is!
And maybe... maybe then, someone will treat me like I matter...

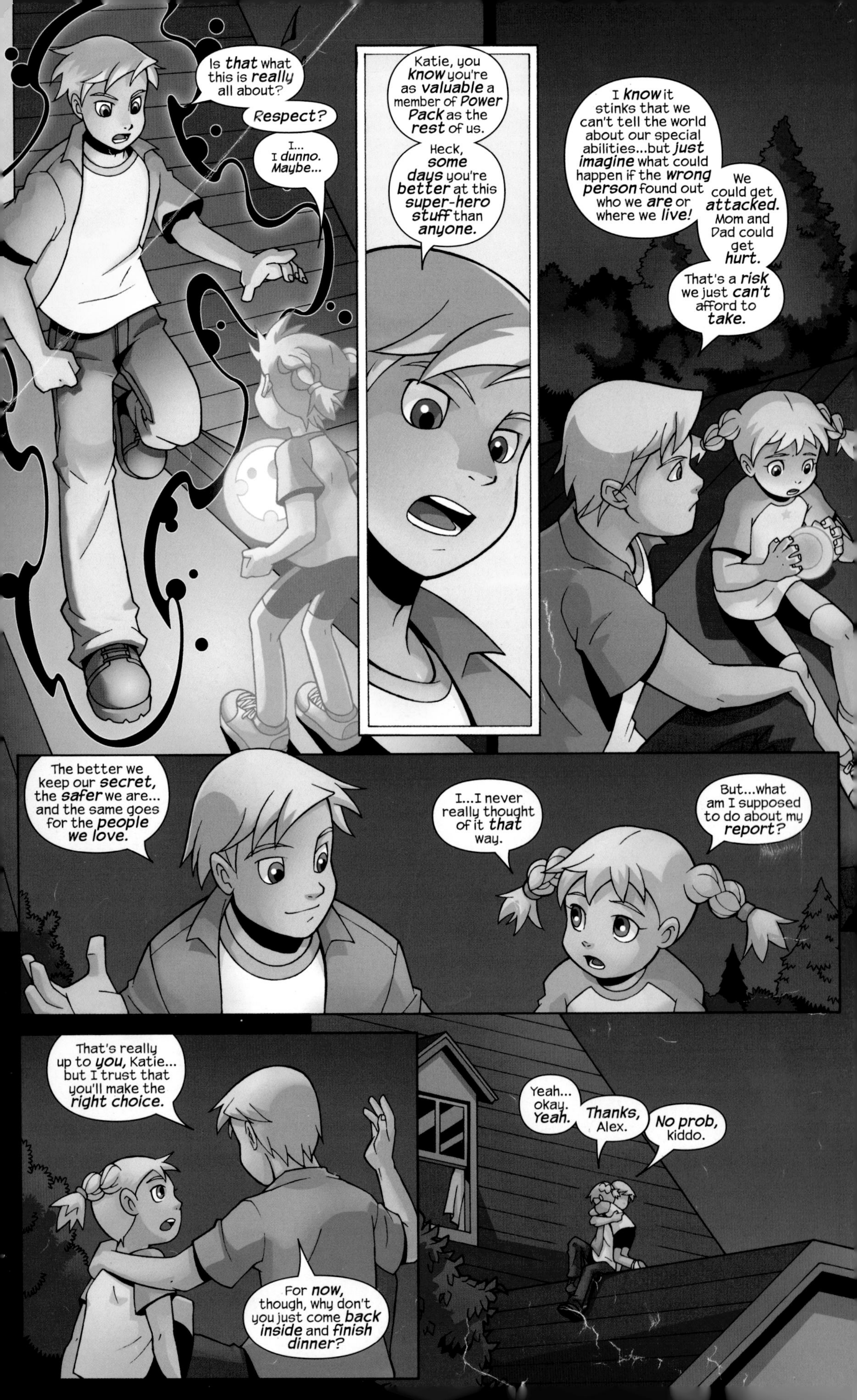
Is *that* what this is *really* all about?
Respect?
I... I *dunno.* Maybe...
Katie, you *know* you're as *valuable* a member of *Power Pack* as the *rest* of us.
Heck, *some days* you're *better* at this *super-hero stuff* than *anyone.*
I *know* it stinks that we can't tell the world about our special abilities...but *just imagine* what could happen if the *wrong person* found out who we *are* or where we *live!*
We could get *attacked.* Mom and Dad could get *hurt.*
That's a *risk* we just *can't* afford to *take.*
The better we keep our *secret,* the *safer* we are... and the same goes for the *people we love.*
I...I never really thought of it *that* way.
But...what am I supposed to do about my *report?*
That's really up to *you,* Katie... but I trust that you'll make the *right choice.*
For *now,* though, why don't you just come *back inside* and *finish dinner?*
Yeah... okay. *Yeah.*
Thanks, Alex.
No prob, kiddo.

FINALLY!

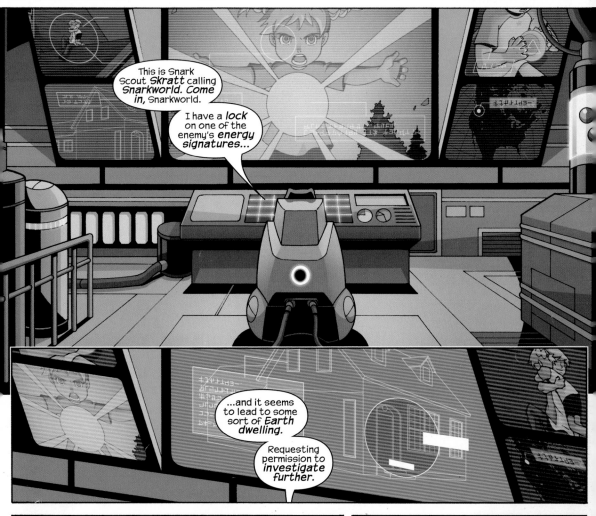

This is Snark Scout *Skratt* calling *Snarkworld. Come in,* Snarkworld.

I have a *lock* on one of the enemy's *energy signatures...*

...and it seems to lead to some sort of *Earth* dwelling.

Requesting permission to *investigate further.*

Permission *denied.* You will *wait* for a support *team* to arrive.

Your *youth* and *inexperience* make you--

No! *Please,* let me handle this one. Let me *prove* my *worth* to the Queen!

I...I *promise* I won't screw it up like *last time,* Dad...

...

Permission *granted.*

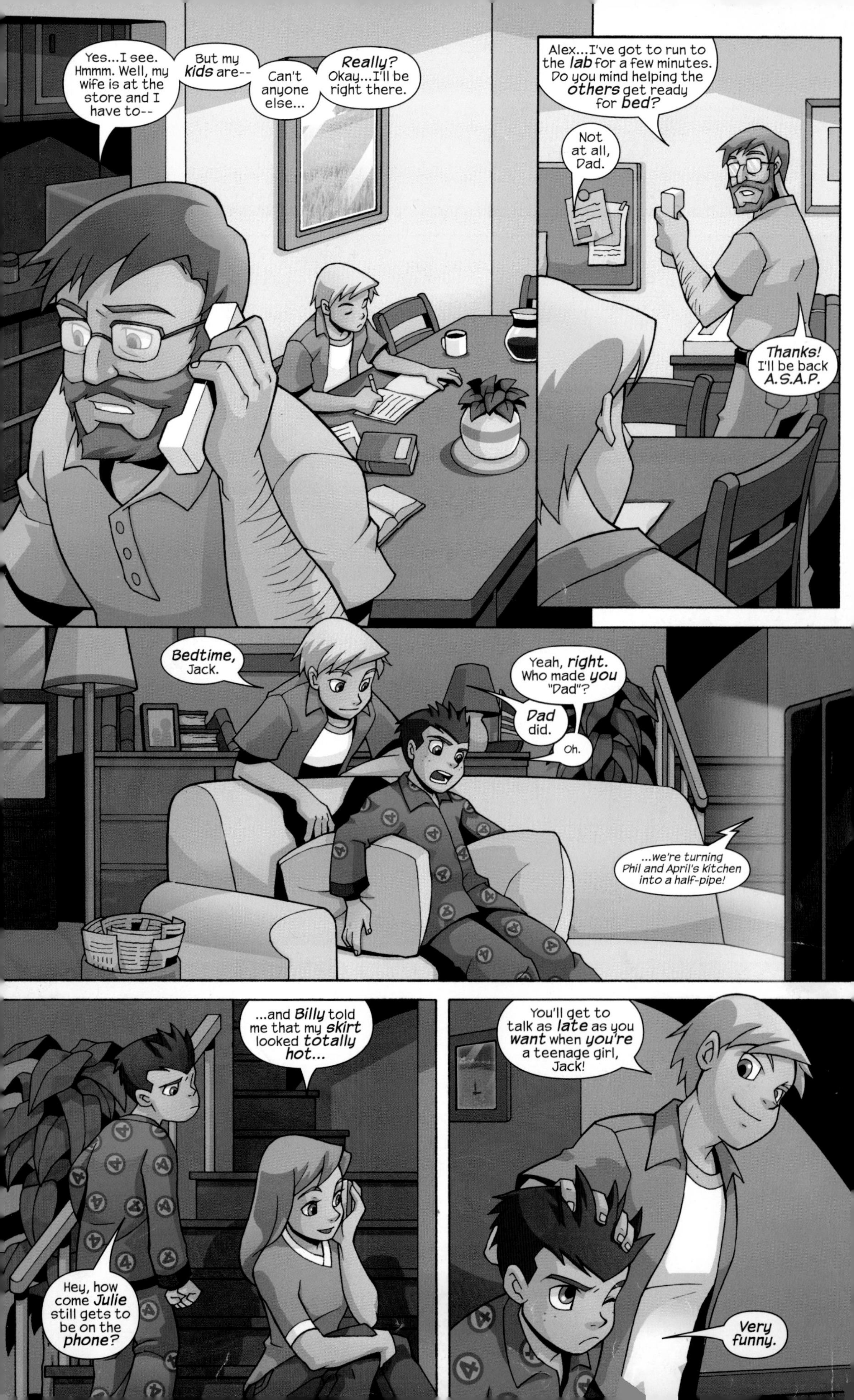
Yes...I see. Hmmm. Well, my wife is at the store and I have to--
But my kids are--
Can't anyone else...
Really? Okay...I'll be right there.
Alex...I've got to run to the lab for a few minutes. Do you mind helping the others get ready for bed?
Not at all, Dad.
Thanks! I'll be back A.S.A.P.
Bedtime, Jack.
Yeah, right. Who made you "Dad"?
Dad did.
Oh.
...we're turning Phil and April's kitchen into a half-pipe!
...and Billy told me that my skirt looked totally hot...
Hey, how come Julie still gets to be on the phone?
You'll get to talk as late as you want when you're a teenage girl, Jack!
Very funny.

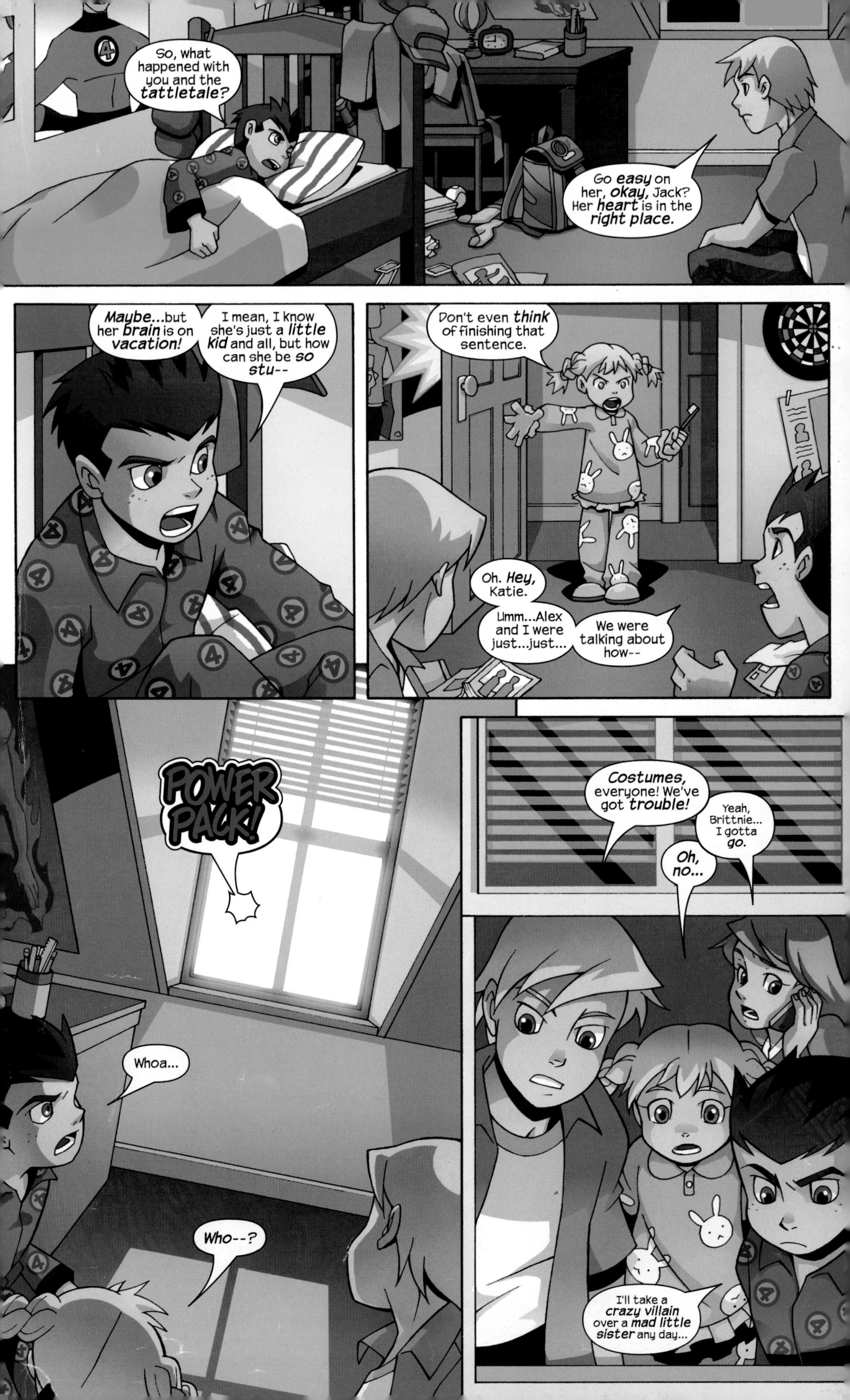
So, what happened with you and the tattletale?
Go easy on her, okay, Jack? Her heart is in the right place.
Maybe...but her brain is on vacation!
I mean, I know she's just a little kid and all, but how can she be so stu--
Don't even think of finishing that sentence.
Oh. Hey, Katie.
Umm...Alex and I were just...just...
We were talking about how--
POWER PACK!
Whoa...
Who--?
Costumes, everyone! We've got trouble!
Yeah, Brittnie... I gotta go.
Oh, no...
I'll take a crazy villain over a mad little sister any day...

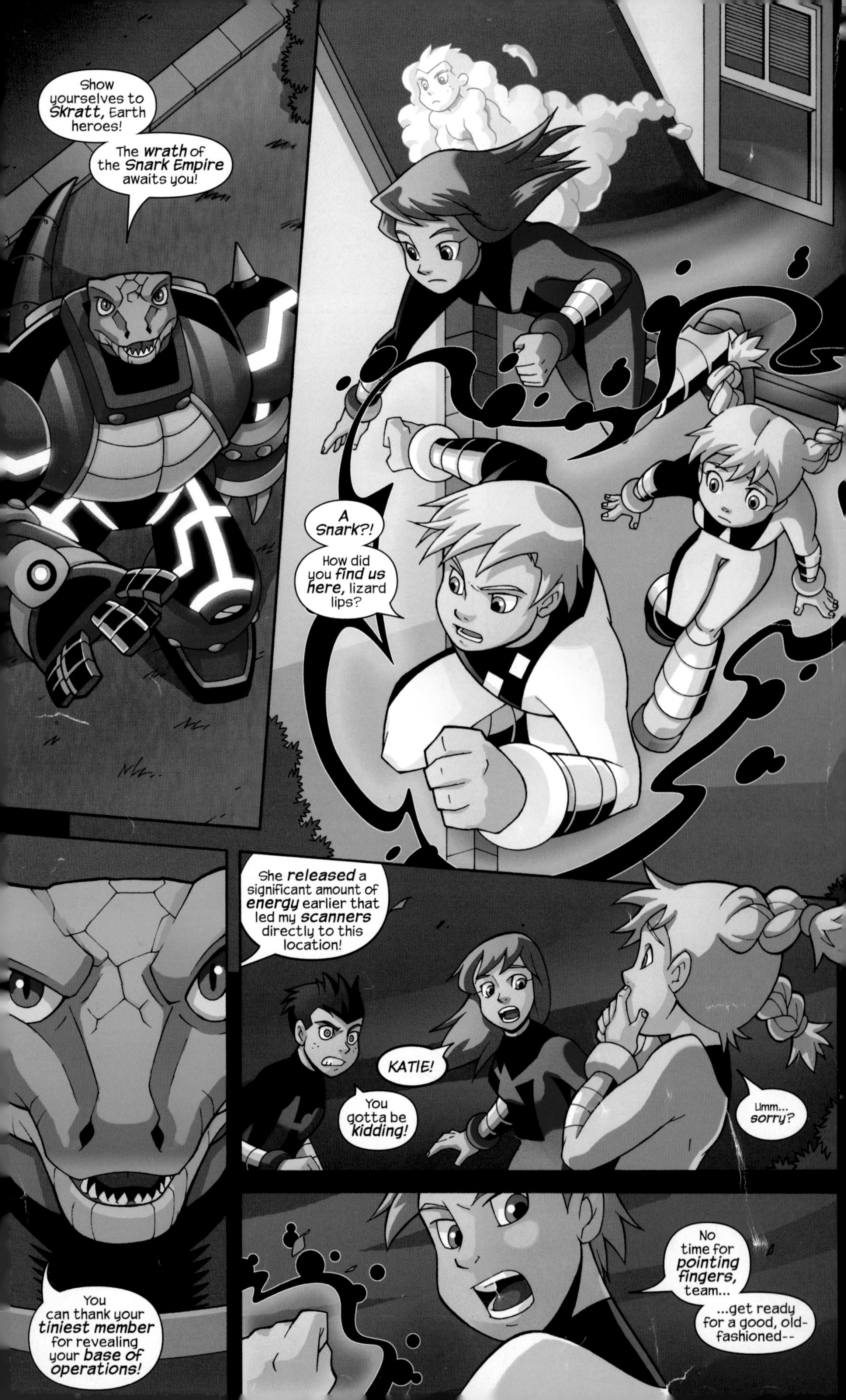
Show yourselves to Skratt, Earth heroes!
The wrath of the Snark Empire awaits you!
A Snark?!
How did you find us here, lizard lips?
She released a significant amount of energy earlier that led my scanners directly to this location!
KATIE!
You gotta be kidding!
Umm... sorry?
You can thank your tiniest member for revealing your base of operations!
No time for pointing fingers, team...
...get ready for a good, old-fashioned--

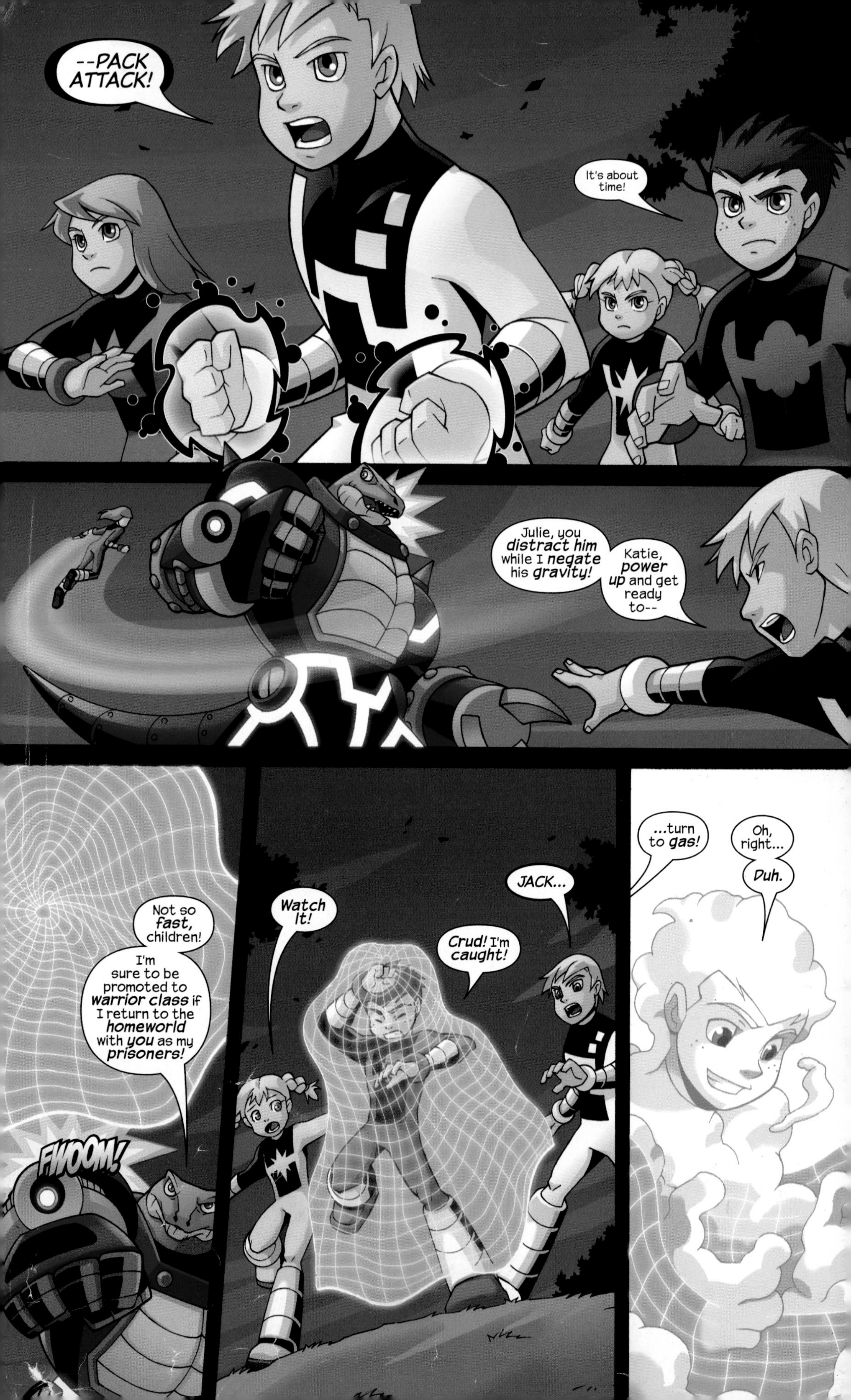
--PACK ATTACK!
It's about time!
Julie, you distract him while I negate his gravity!
Katie, power up and get ready to--
Not so fast, children!
I'm sure to be promoted to warrior class if I return to the homeworld with you as my prisoners!
FWOOM!
Watch It!
Crud! I'm caught!
JACK...
...turn to gas!
Oh, right...
Duh.

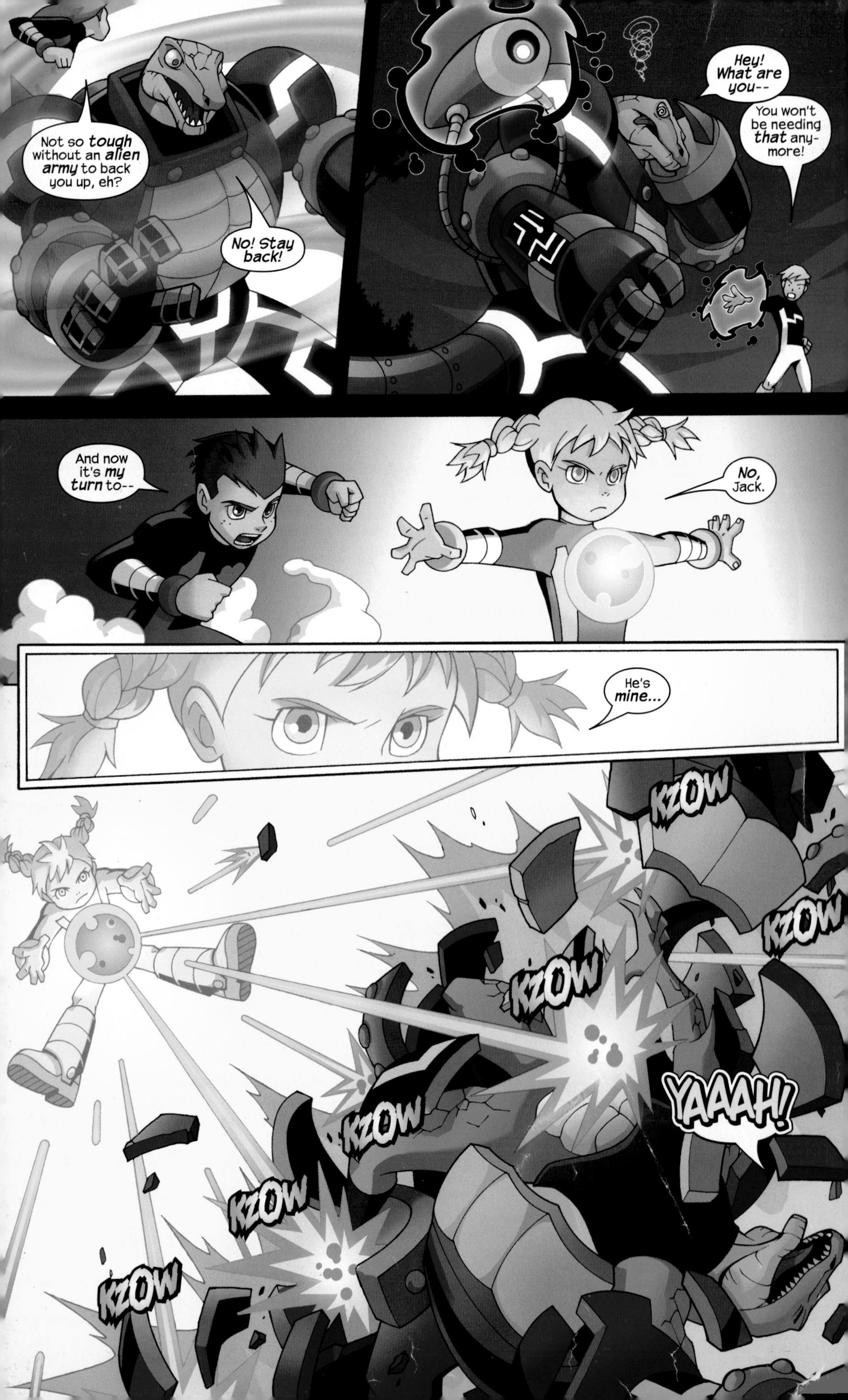
Not so tough without an alien army to back you up, eh?
No! Stay back!
Hey! What are you--
You won't be needing that any-more!
And now it's my turn to--
No, Jack.
He's mine...
KZOW
KZOW
KZOW
KZOW
KZOW
KZOW
YAAAH!

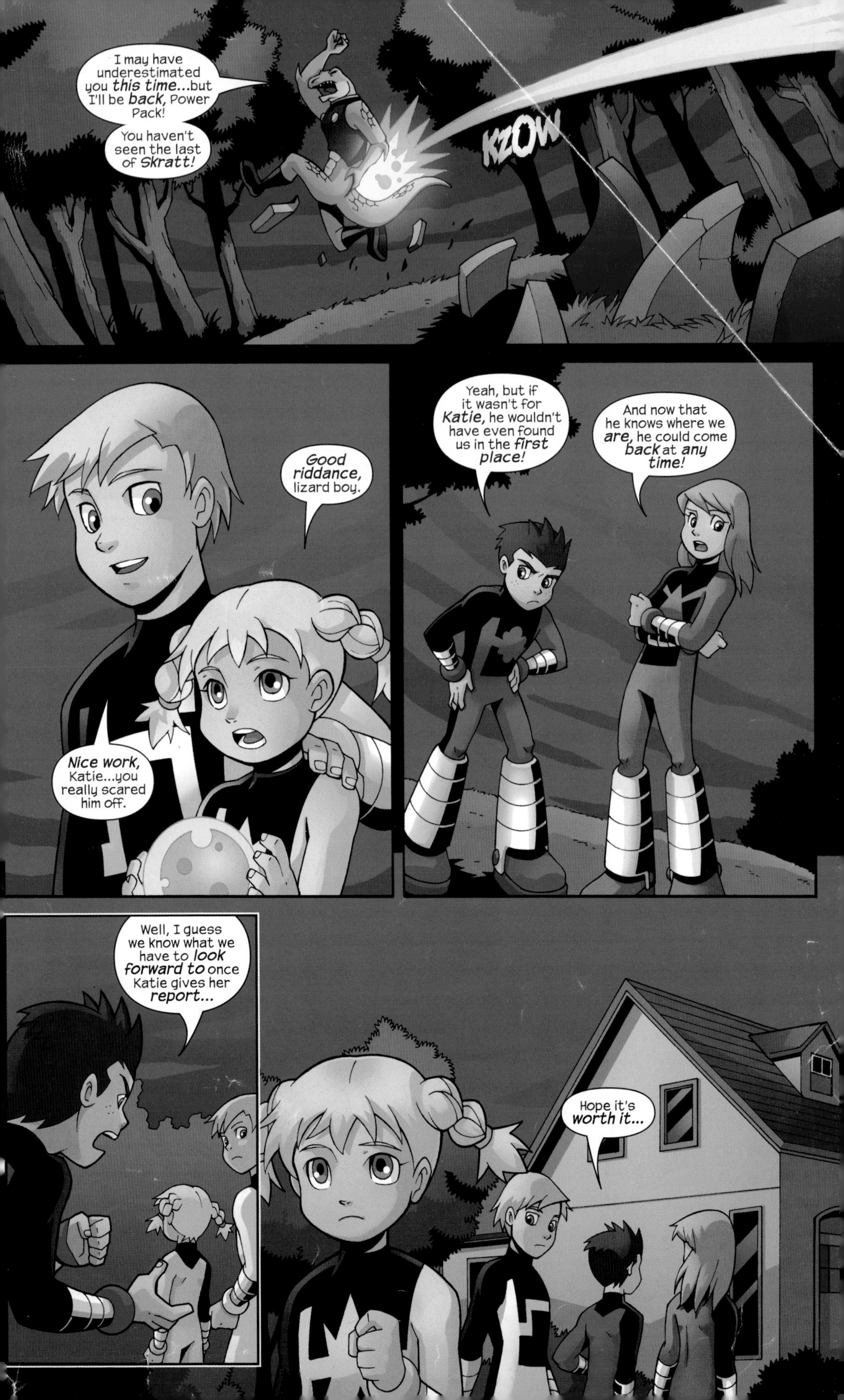

I may have underestimated you this time...but I'll be back, Power Pack!
You haven't seen the last of Skratt!
KZOW
Good riddance, lizard boy.
Nice work, Katie...you really scared him off.
Yeah, but if it wasn't for Katie, he wouldn't have even found us in the first place!
And now that he knows where we are, he could come back at any time!
Well, I guess we know what we have to look forward to once Katie gives her report...
Hope it's worth it...

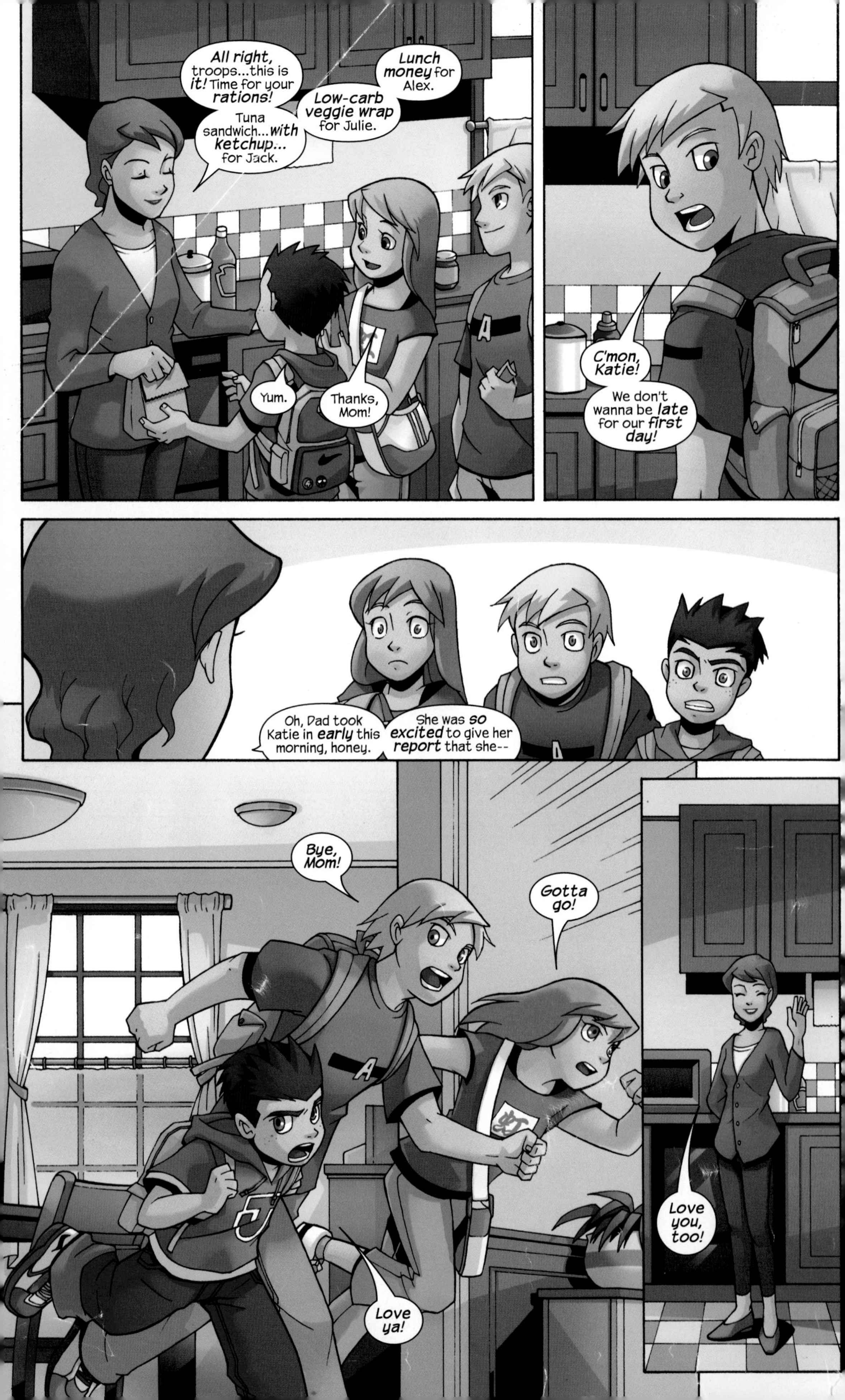

All right, troops...this is it! Time for your rations!
Tuna sandwich...with ketchup... for Jack.
Low-carb veggie wrap for Julie.
Lunch money for Alex.
Yum.
Thanks, Mom!
C'mon, Katie!
We don't wanna be late for our first day!
Oh, Dad took Katie in early this morning, honey.
She was so excited to give her report that she--
Bye, Mom!
Gotta go!
Love ya!
Love you, too!

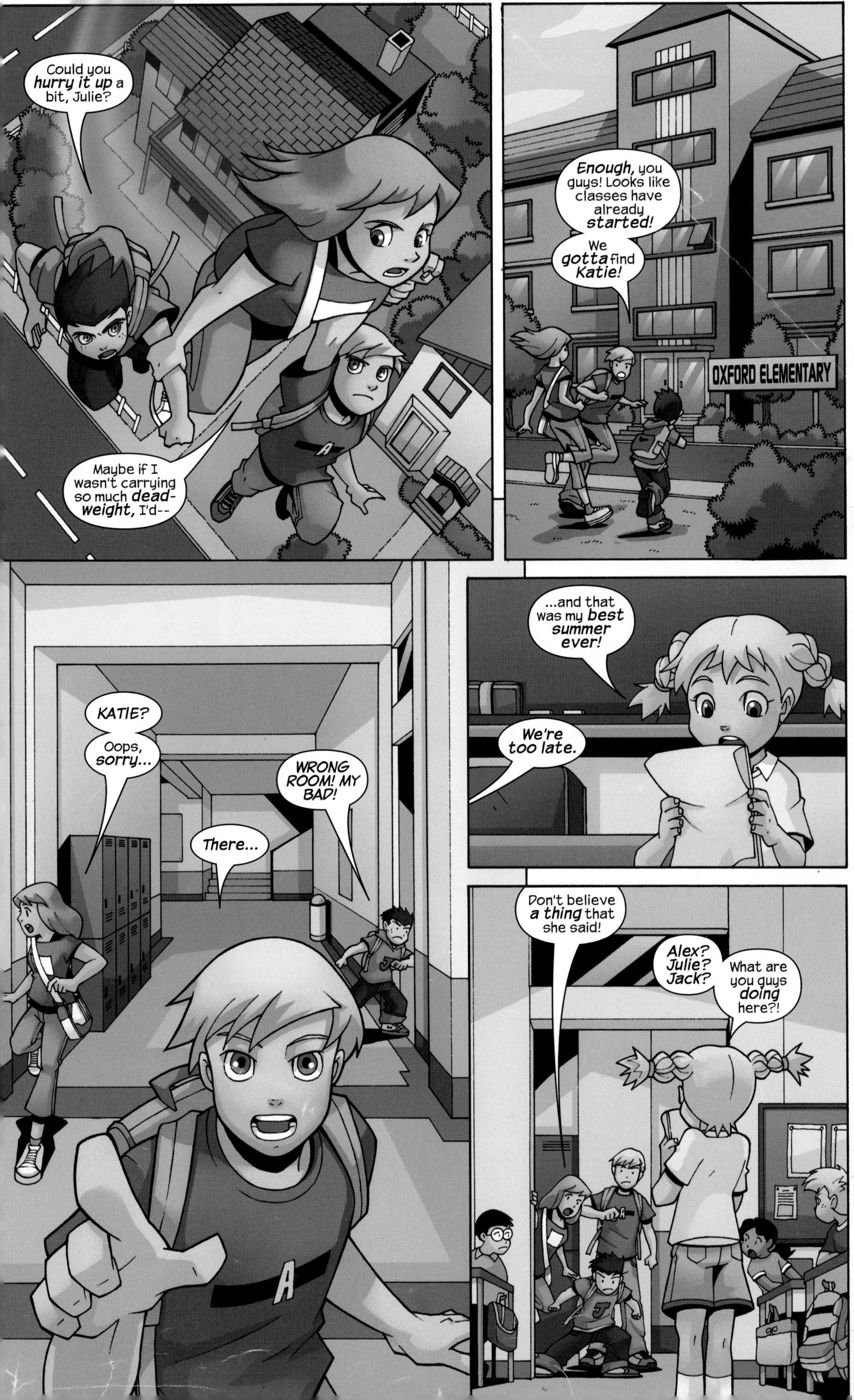
Could you hurry it up a bit, Julie?
Maybe if I wasn't carrying so much dead-weight, I'd--
Enough, you guys! Looks like classes have already started!
We gotta find Katie!
OXFORD ELEMENTARY
KATIE?
Oops, sorry...
WRONG ROOM! MY BAD!
There...
...and that was my best summer ever!
We're too late.
Don't believe a thing that she said!
Alex? Julie? Jack?
What are you guys doing here?!

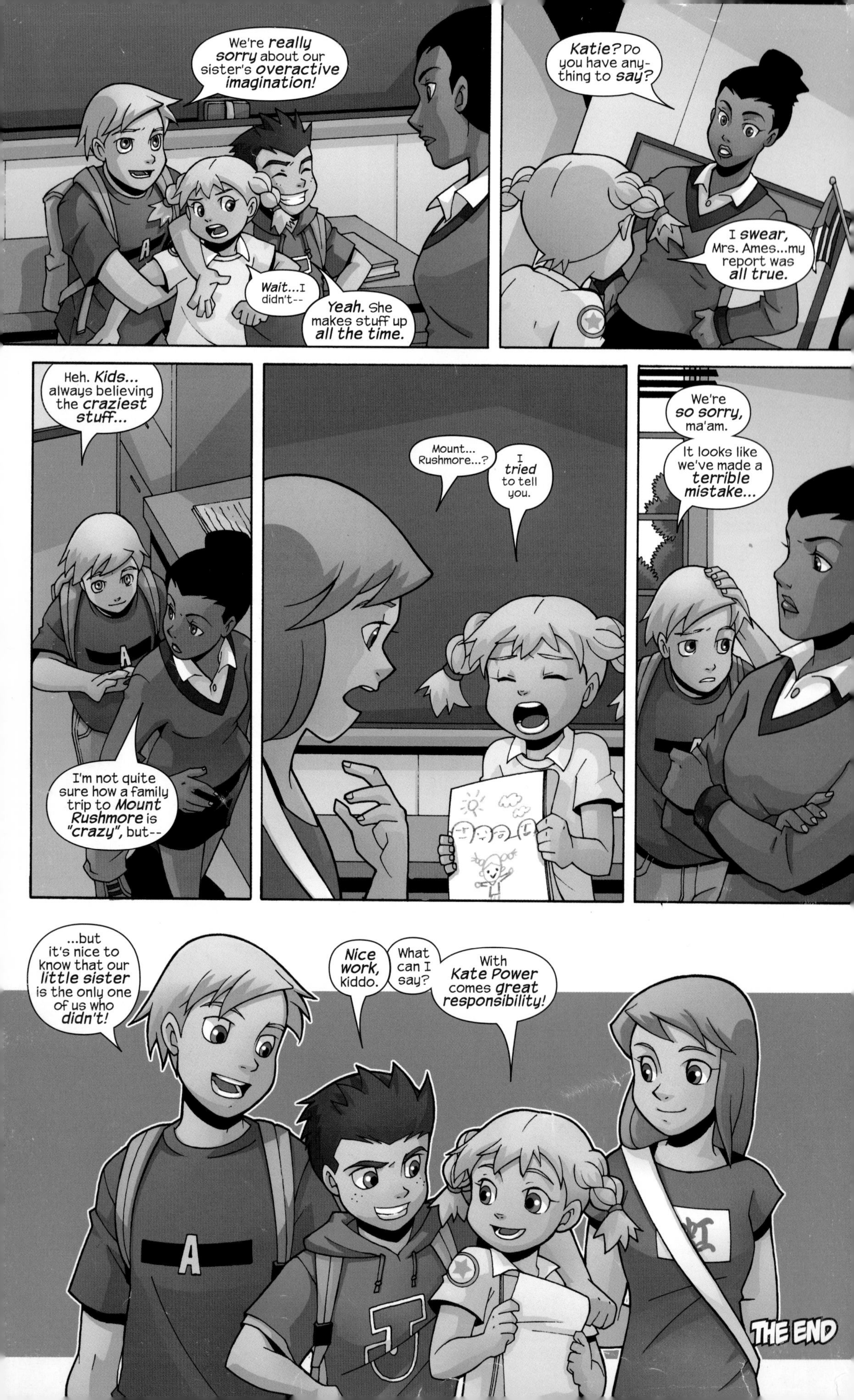

We're really sorry about our sister's overactive imagination!
Wait...I didn't--
Yeah. She makes stuff up all the time.
Katie? Do you have any-thing to say?
I swear, Mrs. Ames...my report was all true.
Heh. Kids... always believing the craziest stuff...
I'm not quite sure how a family trip to Mount Rushmore is "crazy", but--
Mount... Rushmore...?
I tried to tell you.
We're so sorry, ma'am.
It looks like we've made a terrible mistake...
...but it's nice to know that our little sister is the only one of us who didn't!
Nice work, kiddo.
What can I say?
With Kate Power comes great responsibility!
THE END